5/18

AVENGERS K #5
ASSEMBLING THE AVENGERS

When Thor's hammer falls to Earth, S.H.I.E.L.D. Director Nick Fury brings in Agent Clint Barton, A.K.A. Hawkeye, to assist Agent Phil Coulson. Meanwhile, Agent Natasha Romanoff, A.K.A. the Black Widow, has been posing as a student at Culver University, where the Hulk goes on a rampage against the U.S. Army and enhanced soldier Emil Blonsky.

JIM ZUB
SCRIPT

WOO BIN CHOI WITH **JAE SUNG LEE**
ART

MIN JU LEE
INKS

JAE WOONG LEE, HEE YE CHO & IN YOUNG LEE
COLORS

VC's CORY PETIT
LETTERS

WOO BIN CHOI WITH **JAE SUNG LEE, MIN JU LEE, JAE WOONG LEE & HEE YE CHO**
COVER ART

Adapted from *MARVEL'S AVENGERS PRELUDE: FURY'S BIG WEEK #1-4.*
Adaptations written by SI YEON PARK and translated by JI EUN PARK

AVENGERS created by STAN LEE and JACK KIRBY

Original comics written by CHRIS YOST and ERIC PEARSON;
and illustrated by LUKE ROSS, DANIEL HOR, AGUSTIN PADILLA, DON HO,
WELLINTON ALVES, RICK KETCHAM, MARK PENNINGTON and CHRIS SOTOMAYOR

Editor SARAH BRUNSTAD
Manager, Licensed Publishing JEFF REINGOLD
VP Brand Management & Development, Asia C.B. CEBULSKI
VP Production & Special Projects JEFF YOUNGQUIST
SVP Print, Sales & Marketing DAVID GABRIEL
Associate Manager, Digital Assets JOE HOCHSTEIN
Associate Managing Editor KATERI WOODY
Assistant Editor CAITLIN O'CONNELL
Senior Editor, Special Projects JENNIFER GRÜNWALD
Editor, Special Projects MARK D. BEAZLEY
Book Designer: ADAM DEL RE

Editor In Chief AXEL ALONSO
Chief Creative Officer JOE QUESADA
President DAN BUCKLEY
Executive Producer ALAN FINE

MARVEL

ABDO
Spotlight

AVENGERS ACTIVE ROSTER

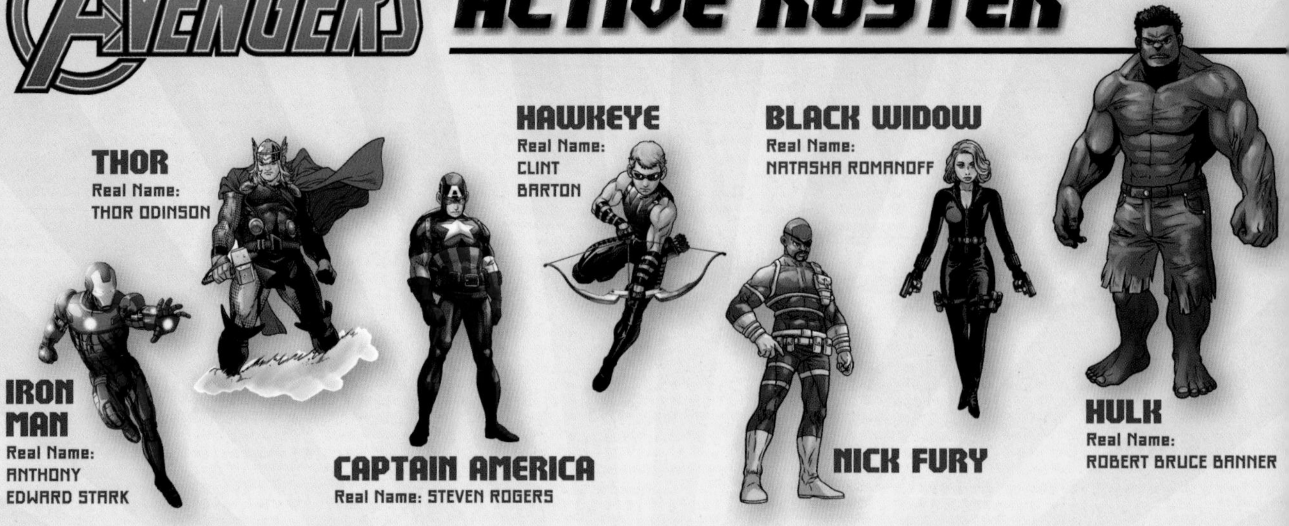
THOR
Real Name: THOR ODINSON
HAWKEYE
Real Name: CLINT BARTON
BLACK WIDOW
Real Name: NATASHA ROMANOFF
IRON MAN
Real Name: ANTHONY EDWARD STARK
CAPTAIN AMERICA
Real Name: STEVEN ROGERS
NICK FURY
HULK
Real Name: ROBERT BRUCE BANNER

EXTRAORDINARY ALLIES

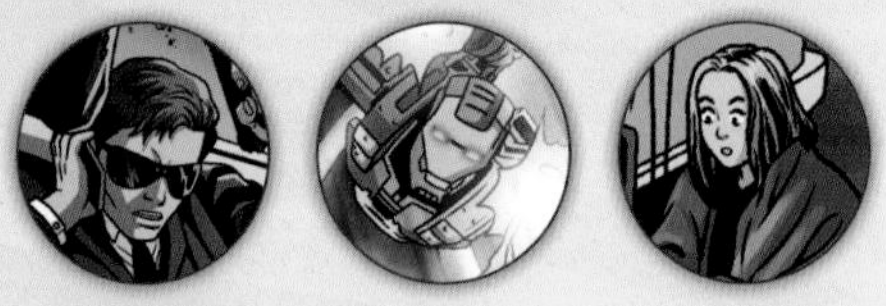

PHIL COULSON | WAR MACHINE | JANE FOSTER

AVENGERS MOST WANTED

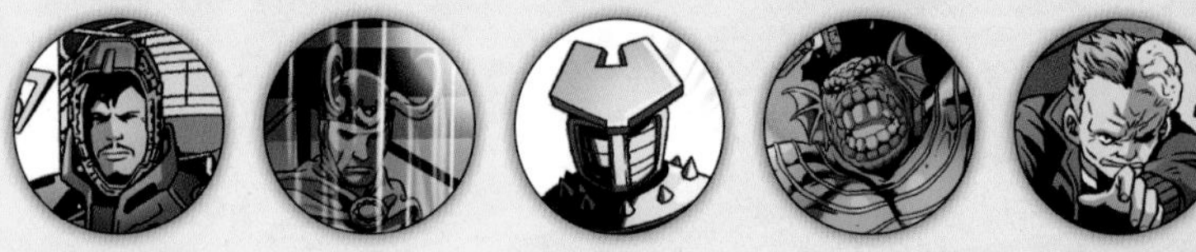

WHIPLASH | LOKI | DESTROYER | ABOMINATION | SAMUEL STERNS

ABDOPUBLISHING.COM

Reinforced library bound edition published in 2018 by Spotlight, a division of ABDO, PO Box 398166, Minneapolis, Minnesota 55439.
Spotlight produces high-quality reinforced library bound editions for schools and libraries. Published by agreement with Marvel Characters, Inc.
Printed in the United States of America, North Mankato, Minnesota.
092017 012018

MARVEL
marvelkids.com

THIS BOOK CONTAINS RECYCLED MATERIALS

PUBLISHER'S CATALOGING-IN-PUBLICATION DATA

Names: Zub, Jim, author. | Choi, Woo Bin; Lee, Jae Sung; Lee, Min Ju; Lee, Jae Woong; Cho, Hee Ye; Lee, In Young, illustrators.
Title: Assembling the Avengers / writer: Jim Zub ; art: Woo Bin Choi; Jae Sung Lee; Min Ju Lee; Jae Woong Lee; Hee Ye Cho; In Young Lee.
Description: Minneapolis, MN : Spotlight, 2018 | Series: Avengers K Set 3
Summary: With a changing world full of threats bigger than he could imagine, S.H.I.E.L.D. director Nick Fury struggles to follow orders from the World Security Council. He calls upon Agent Coulson, Hawkeye, and Black Widow for aid to search for the missing Captain America, help Tony Stark fix his failing arc reactor in his chest, stop the Hulk from going on a rampage, and unearth an alien object, followed shortly by its electrifying owner.
Identifiers: LCCN 2017941923 | ISBN 9781532141478 (v.1 ; lib. bdg.) | ISBN 9781532141485 (v.2 ; lib. bdg.) | ISBN 9781532141492 (v.3 ; lib. bdg.) | ISBN 9781532141508 (v.4 ; lib. bdg.) | ISBN 9781532141515 (v.5 ; lib. bdg.) | ISBN 9781532141522 (v.6 ; lib. bdg.) | ISBN 9781532141539 (v.7 ; lib.bdg.)
Subjects: LCSH: Avengers (ficitious character)--Juvenile fiction. | Super heroes--Juvenile fiction. | Graphic Novels--Juvenile fiction. | Media Tie-in--Juvenile fiction.
Classification: DDC 741.5--dc23
LC record available at http://lccn.loc.gov/2017941923

ABDO
Spotlight
A Division of ABDO
abdopublishing.com

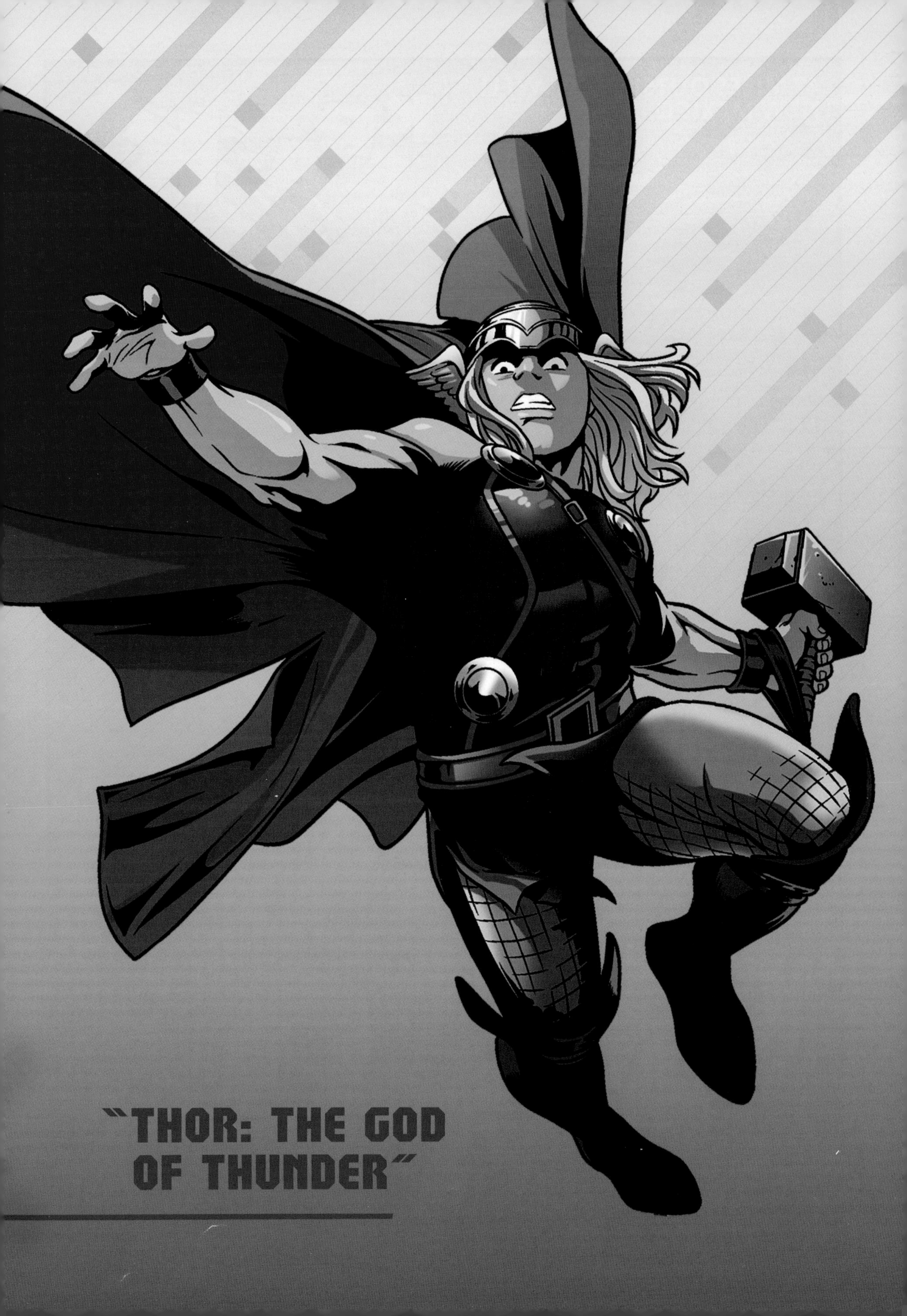

"THOR: THE GOD OF THUNDER"

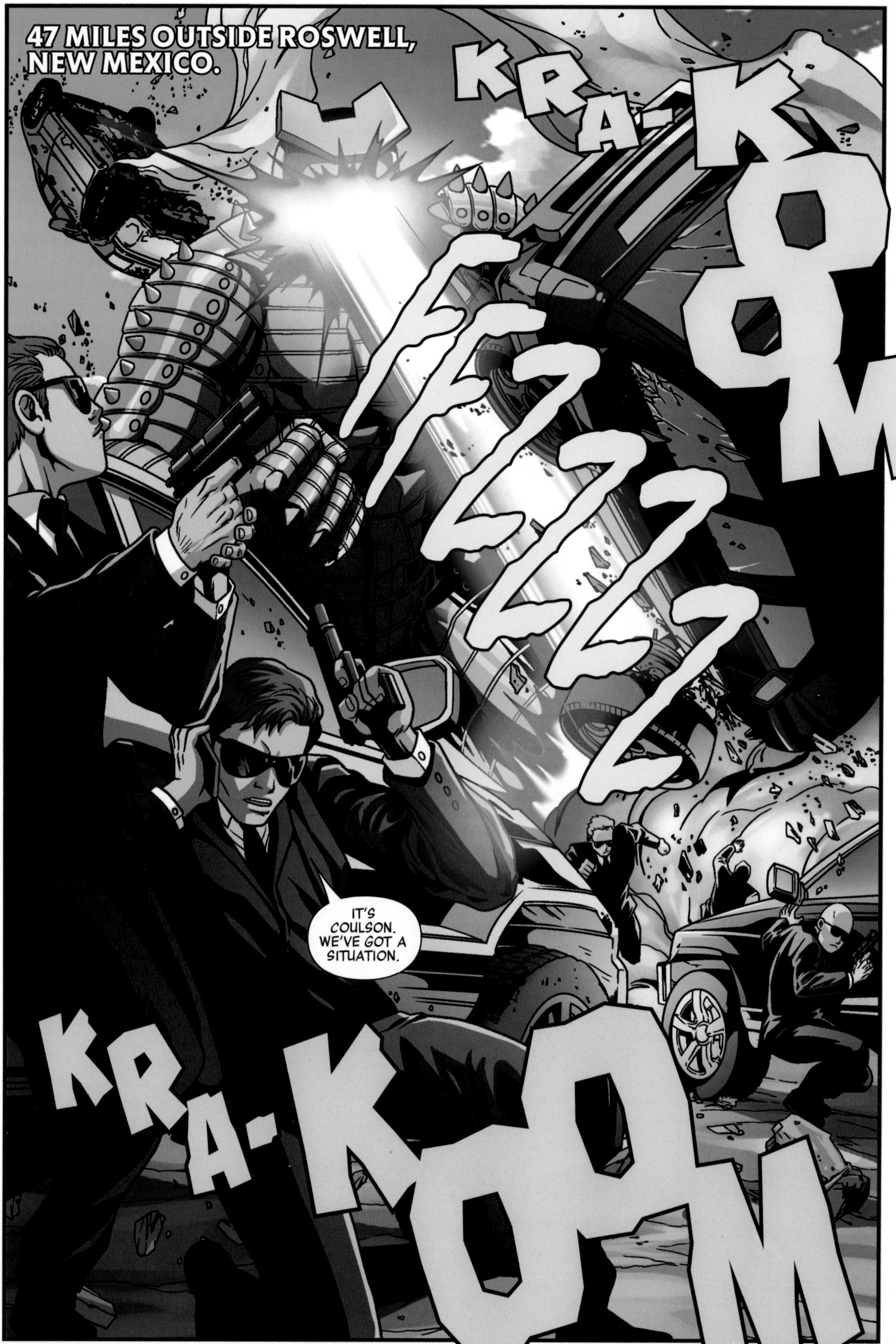
47 MILES OUTSIDE ROSWELL, NEW MEXICO.
KRA-KOOM
FFZZZZ
IT'S COULSON. WE'VE GOT A SITUATION.
KRA-KOOM

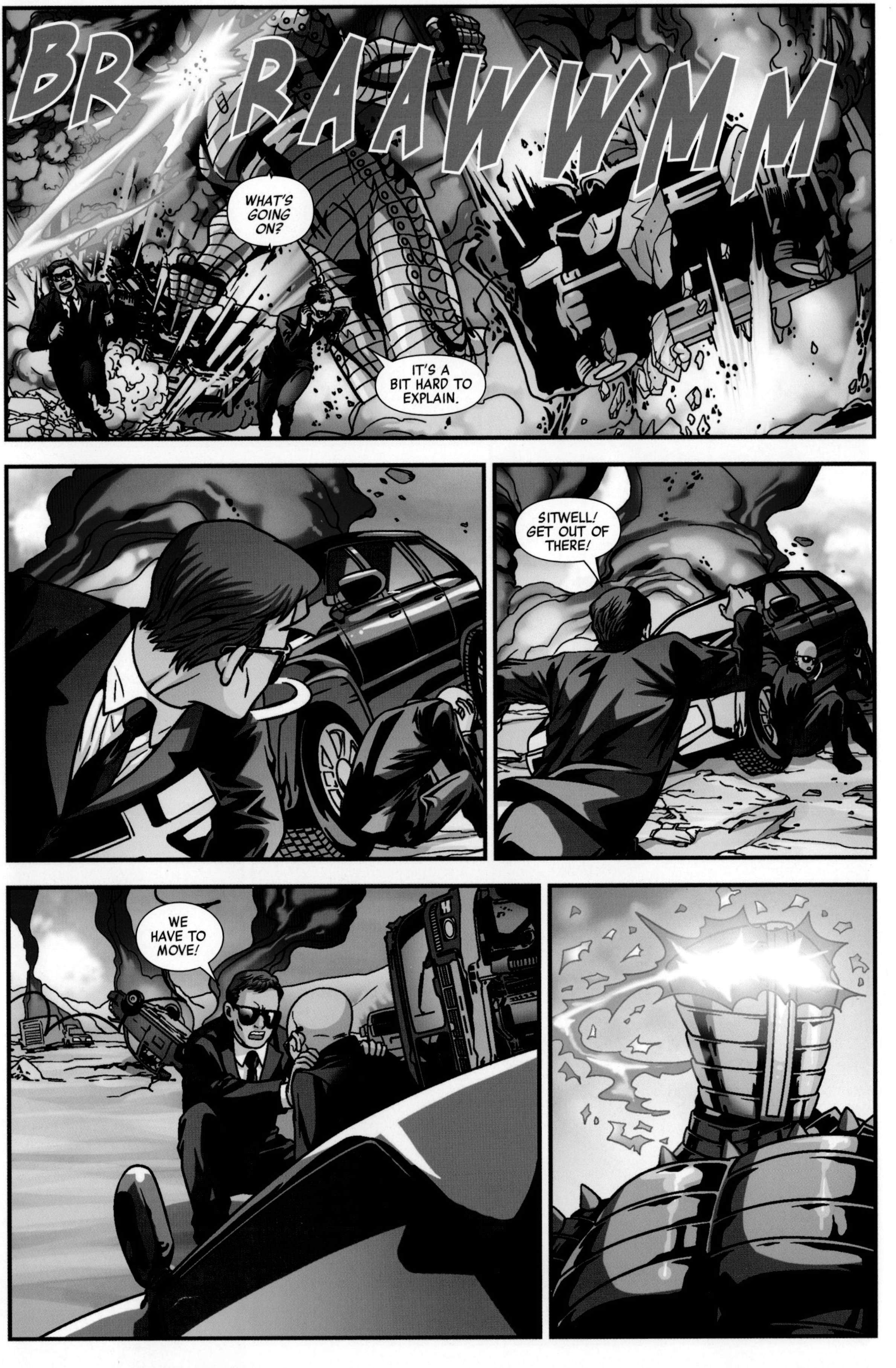
BRRAAWWMM
WHAT'S GOING ON?
IT'S A BIT HARD TO EXPLAIN.
SITWELL! GET OUT OF THERE!
WE HAVE TO MOVE!

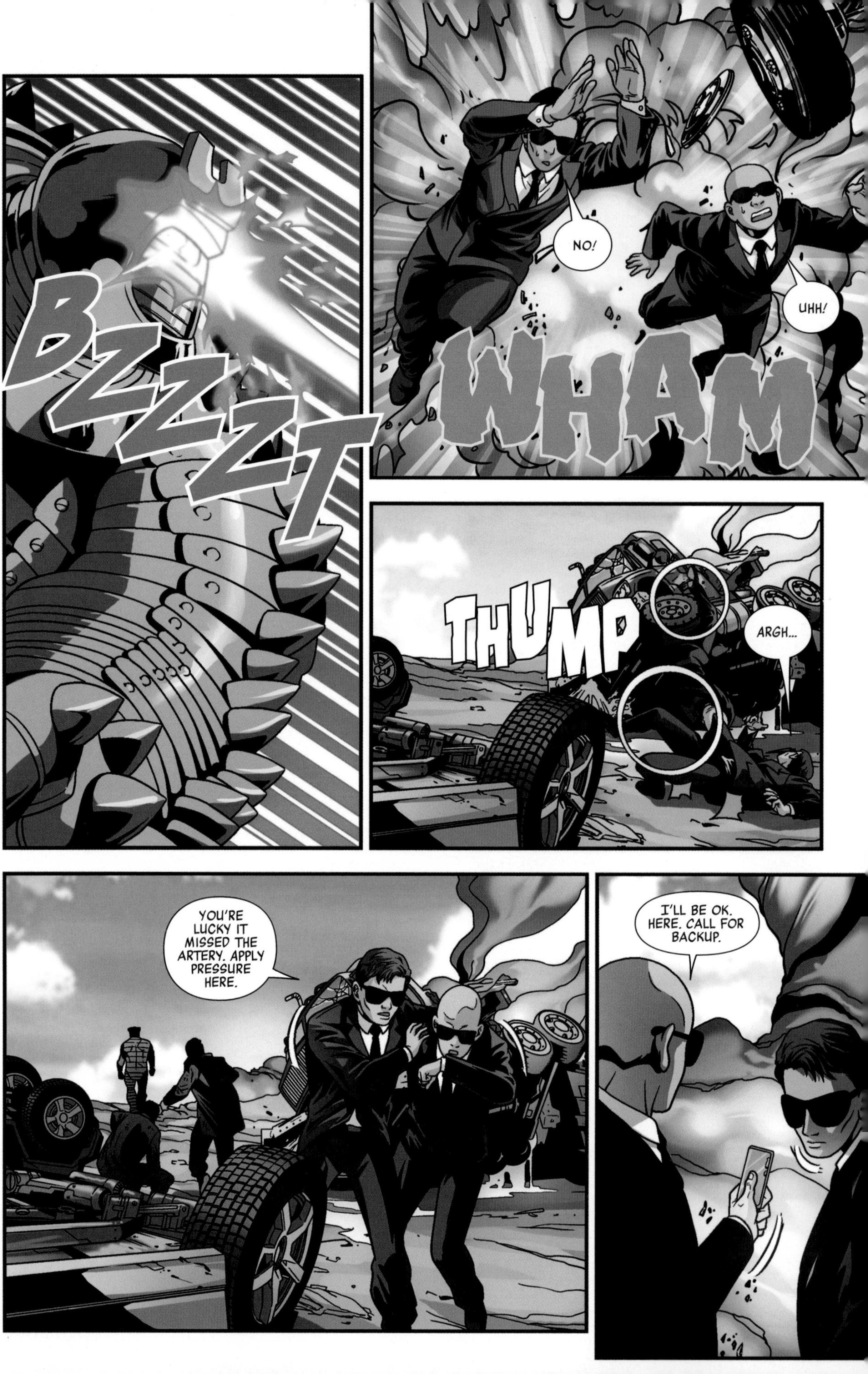
BZZZZT
NO!
UHH!
WHAM
THUMP
ARGH...
YOU'RE LUCKY IT MISSED THE ARTERY. APPLY PRESSURE HERE.
I'LL BE OK. HERE. CALL FOR BACKUP.

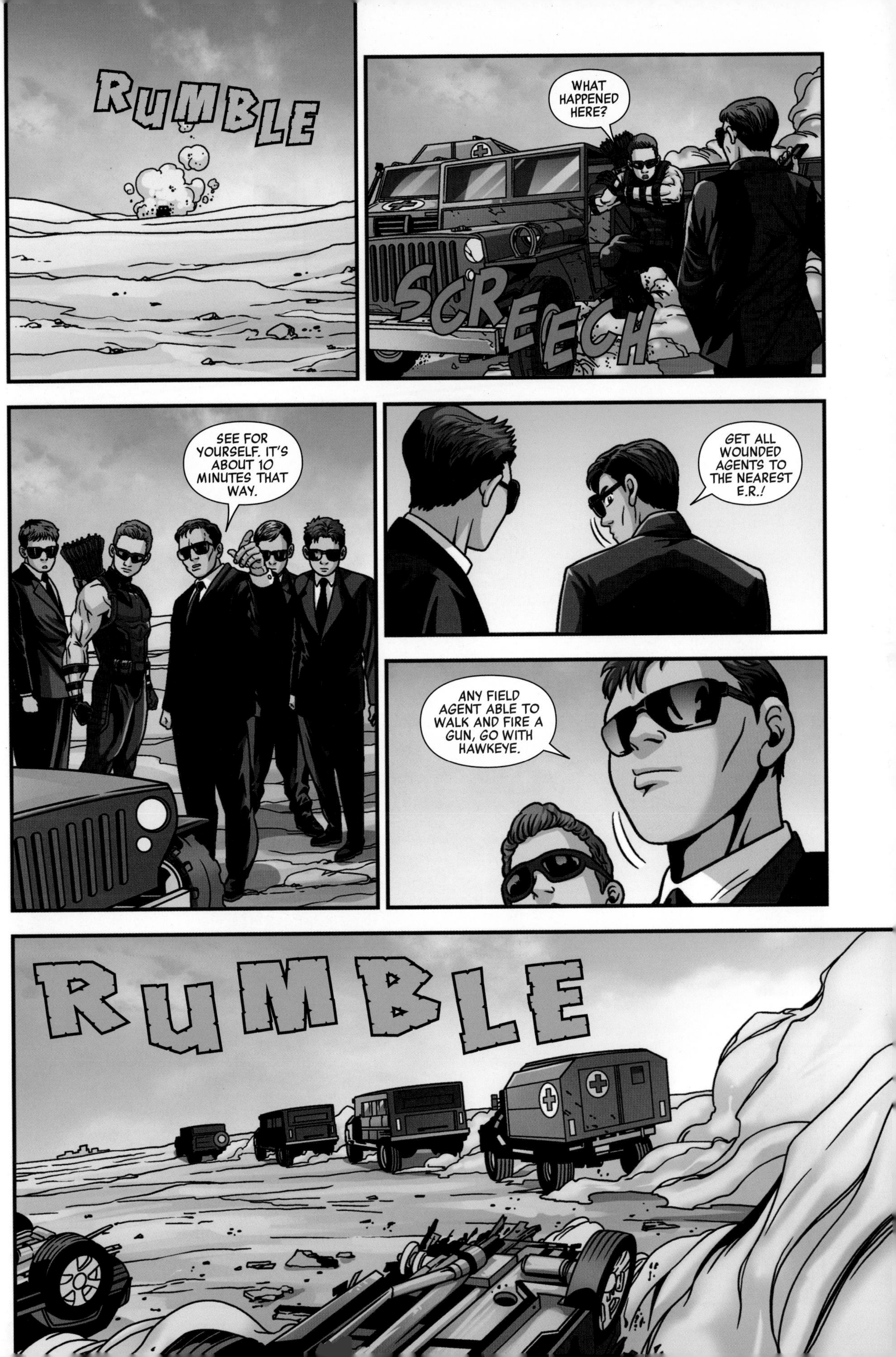
RUMBLE
WHAT HAPPENED HERE?
SCREECH
SEE FOR YOURSELF. IT'S ABOUT 10 MINUTES THAT WAY.
GET ALL WOUNDED AGENTS TO THE NEAREST E.R.!
ANY FIELD AGENT ABLE TO WALK AND FIRE A GUN, GO WITH HAWKEYE.
RUMBLE

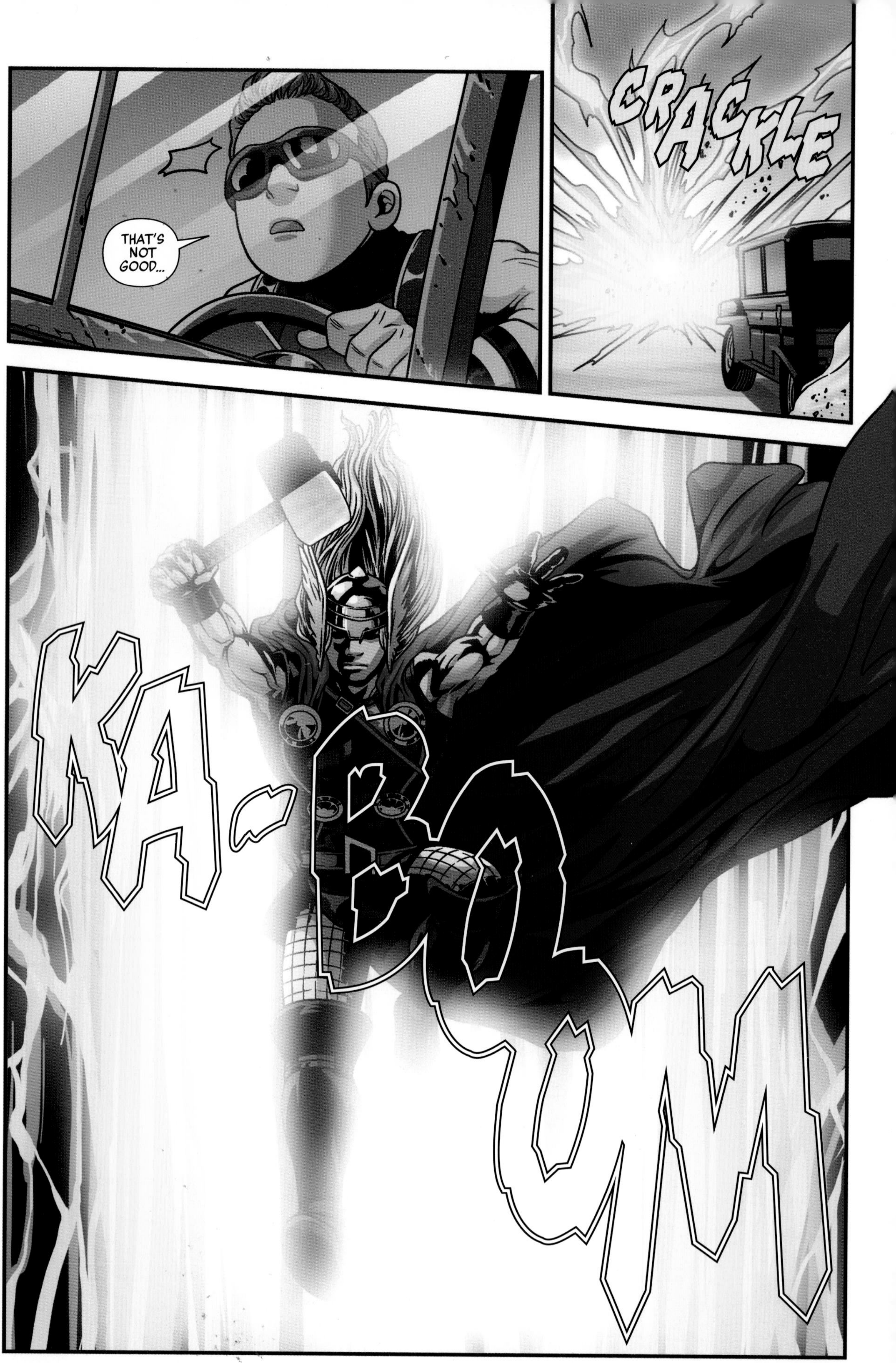
THAT'S NOT GOOD...
CRACKLE
KA-BOOM

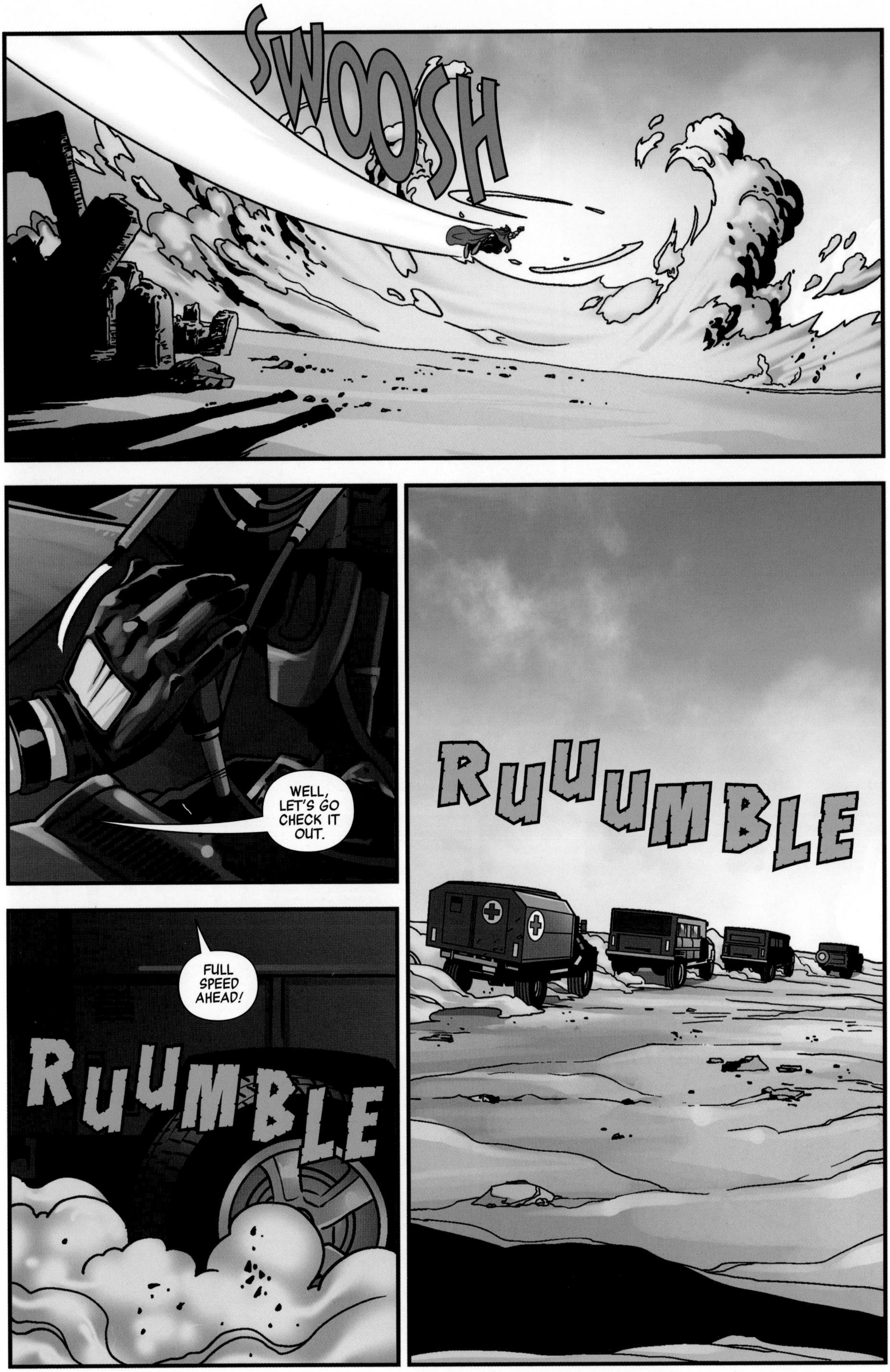
SWOOSH
WELL, LET'S GO CHECK IT OUT.
FULL SPEED AHEAD!
RUUMBLE
RUUUMBLE

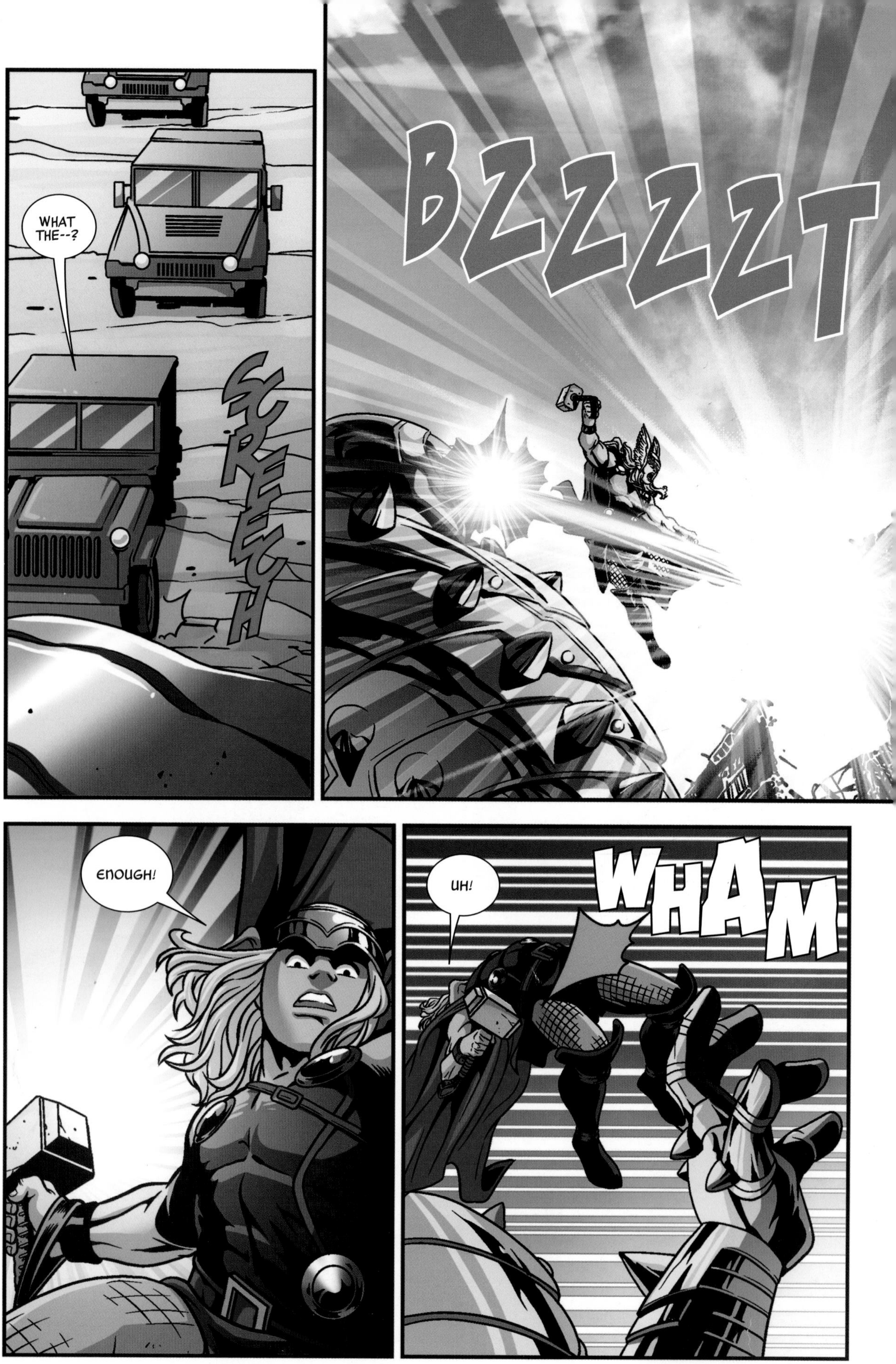
WHAT THE--?
SCREECH
BZZZZZT
ENOUGH!
UH!
WHAM

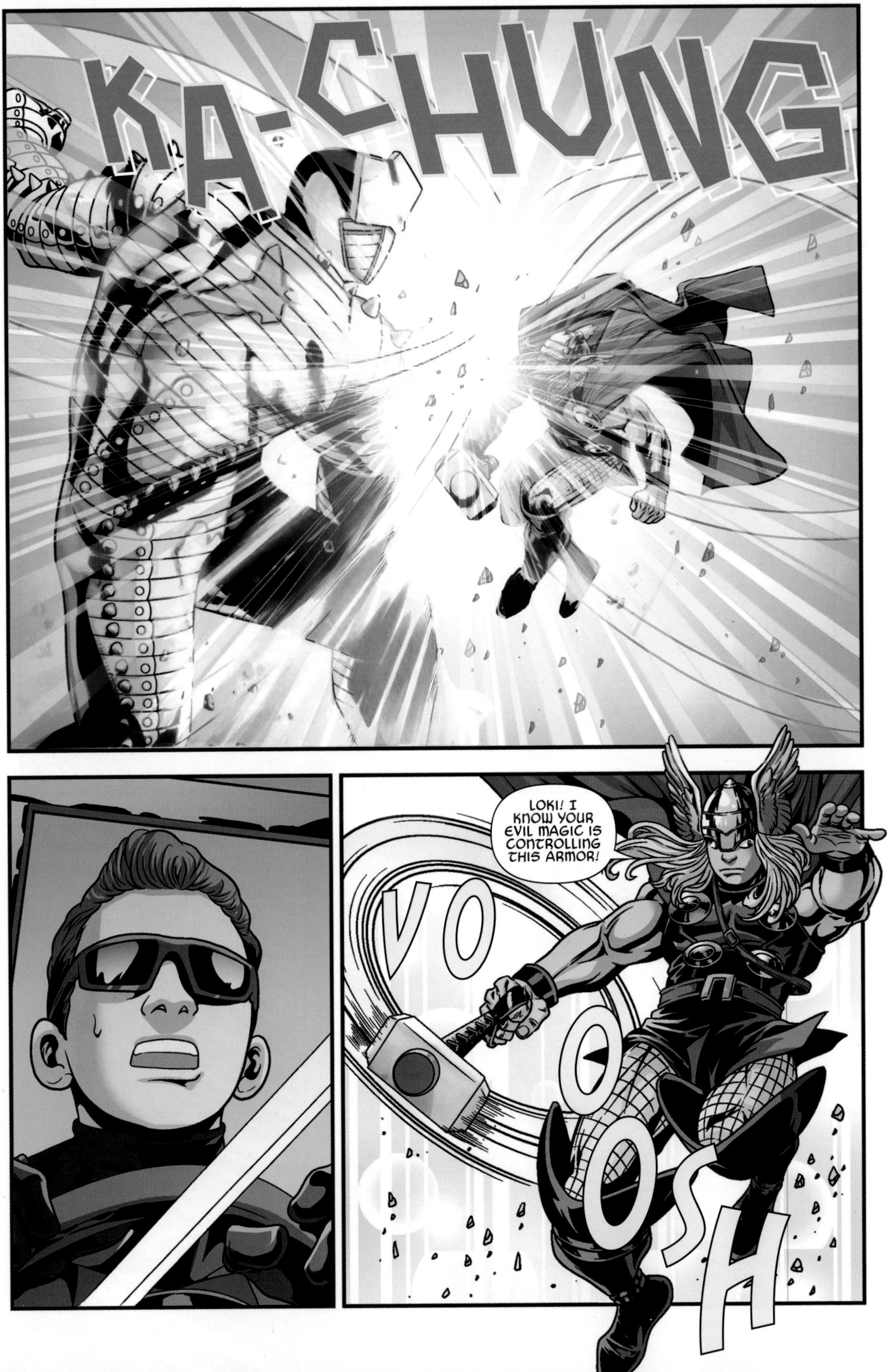
KA-CHUNG
LOKI! I KNOW YOUR EVIL MAGIC IS CONTROLLING THIS ARMOR!
VOOOOSH

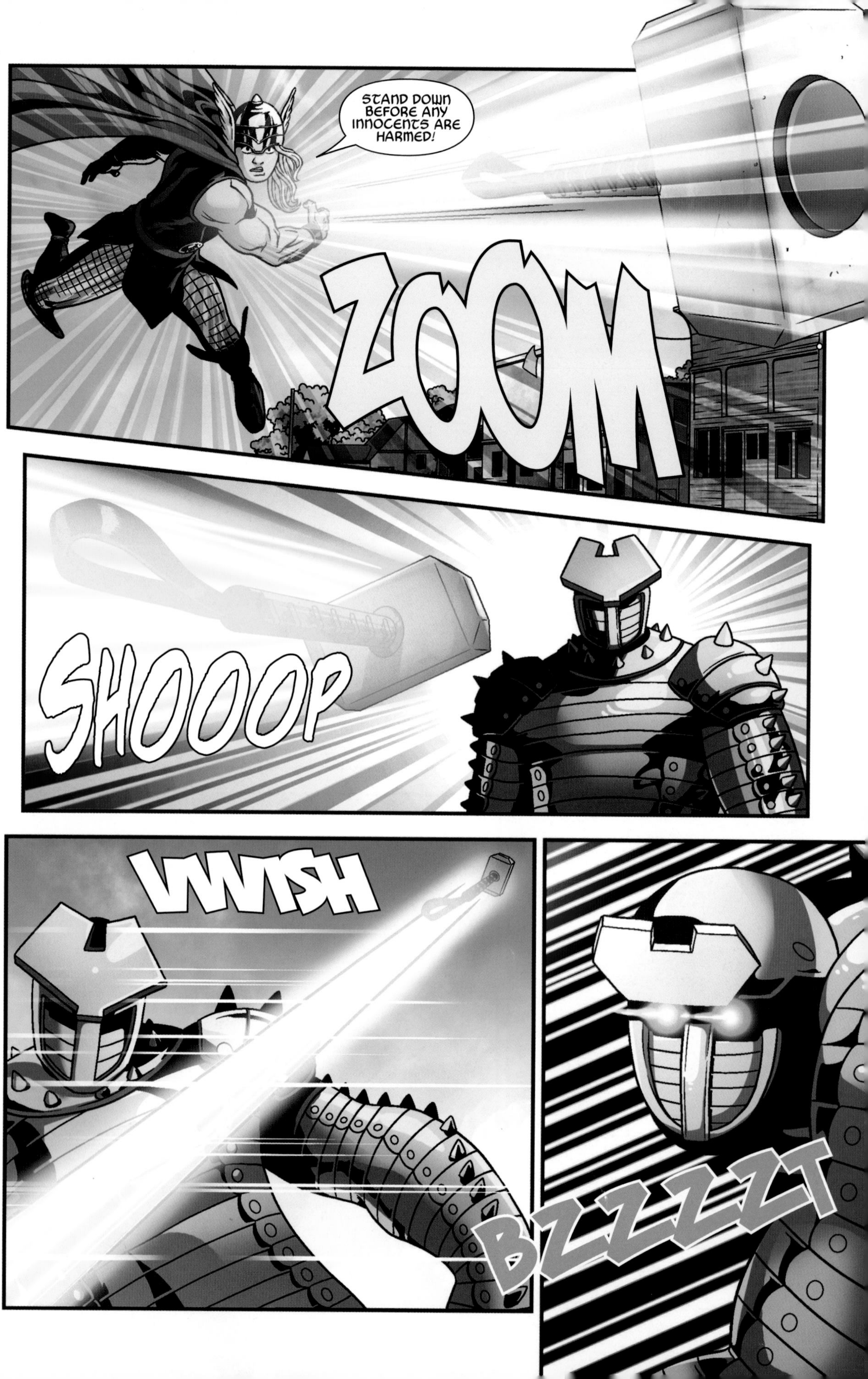
STAND DOWN BEFORE ANY INNOCENTS ARE HARMED!
ZOOM
SHOOOP
VVVISH
BZZZZZT

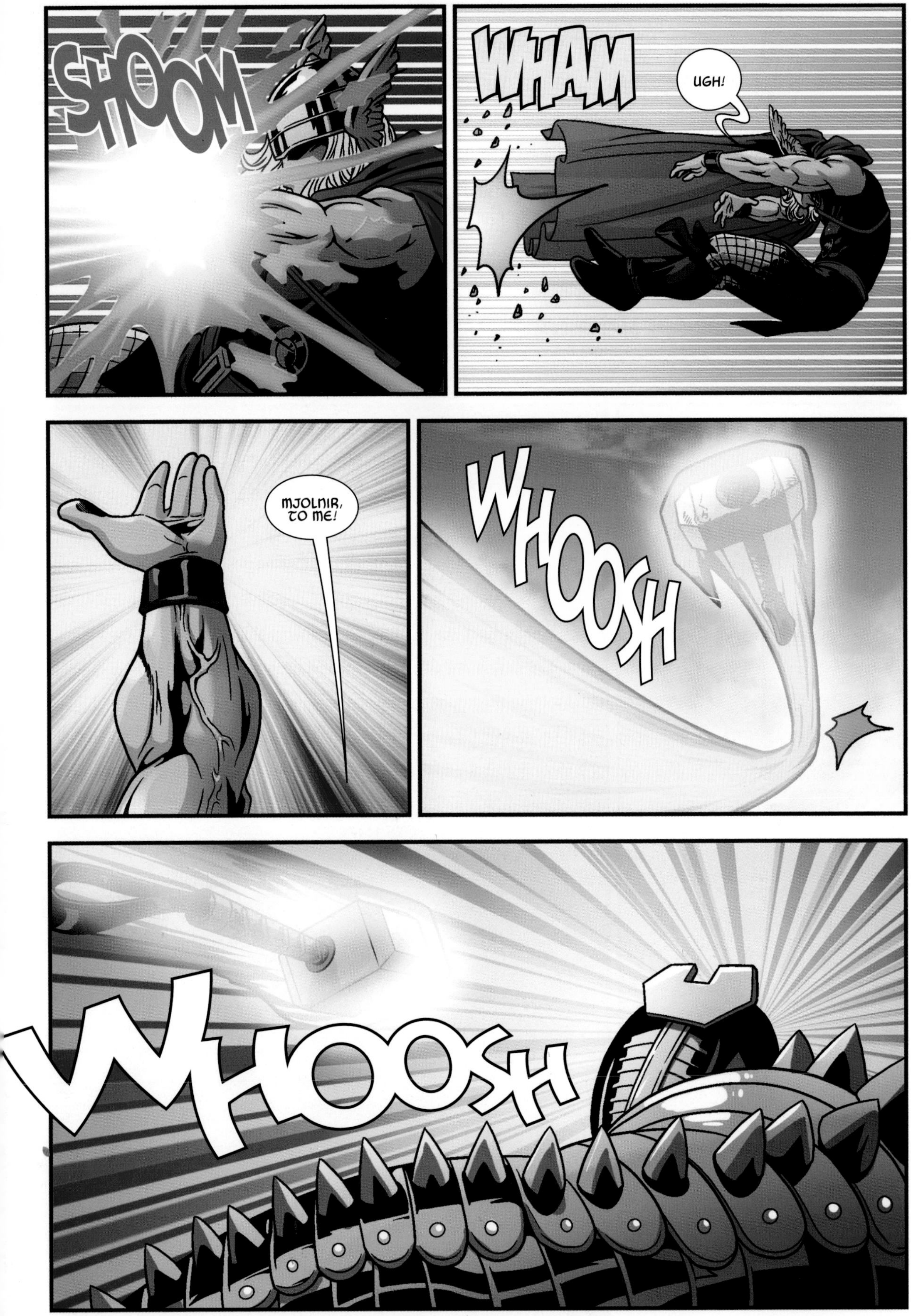
SHOOM
WHAM
UGH!
MJOLNIR, TO ME!
WHOOSH
WHOOSH

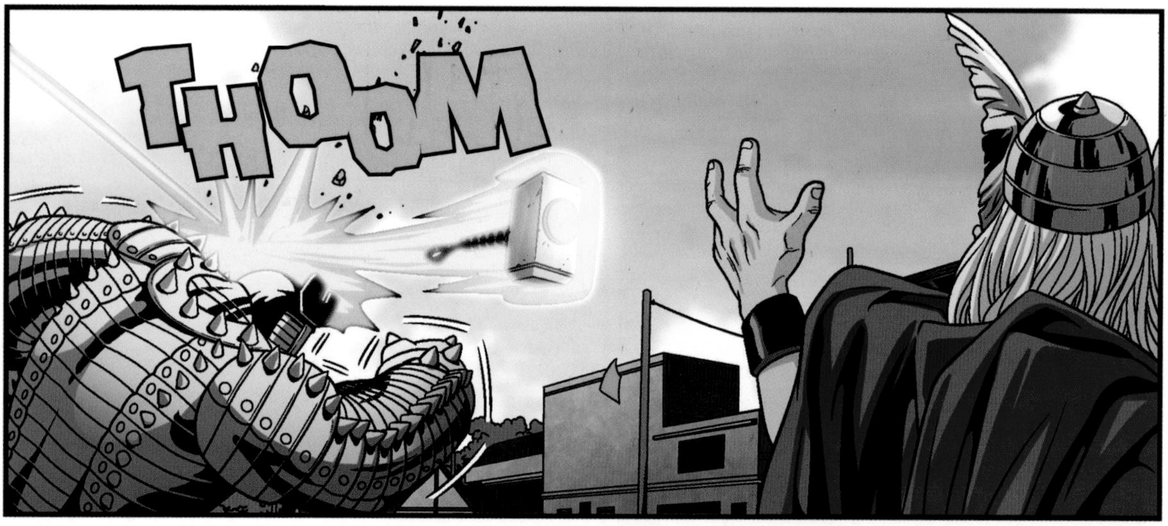
THOOOM

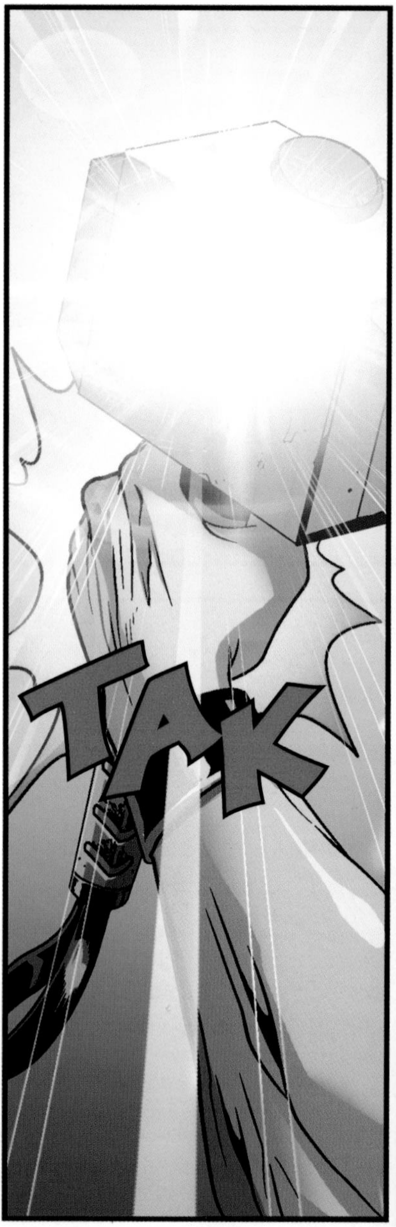
TAK

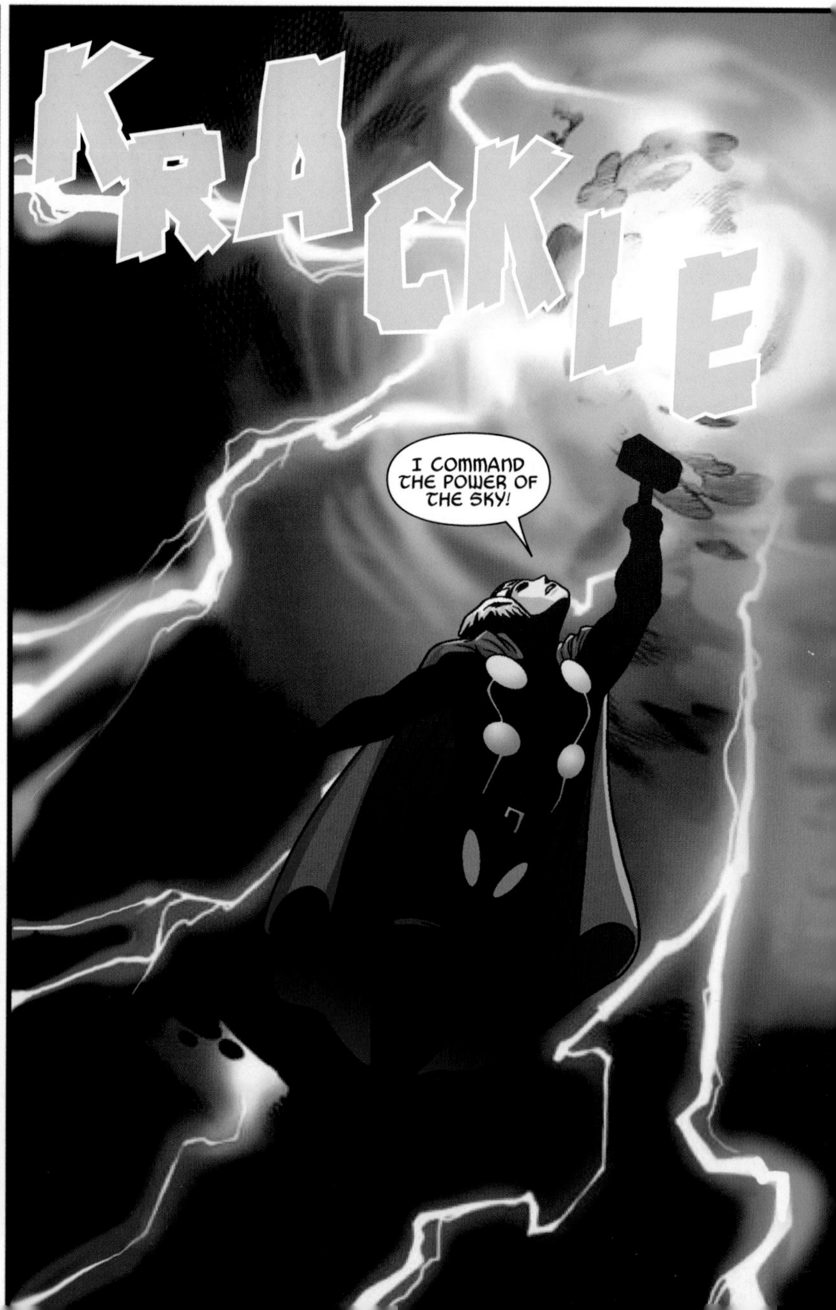
KRACKLE
I COMMAND THE POWER OF THE SKY!

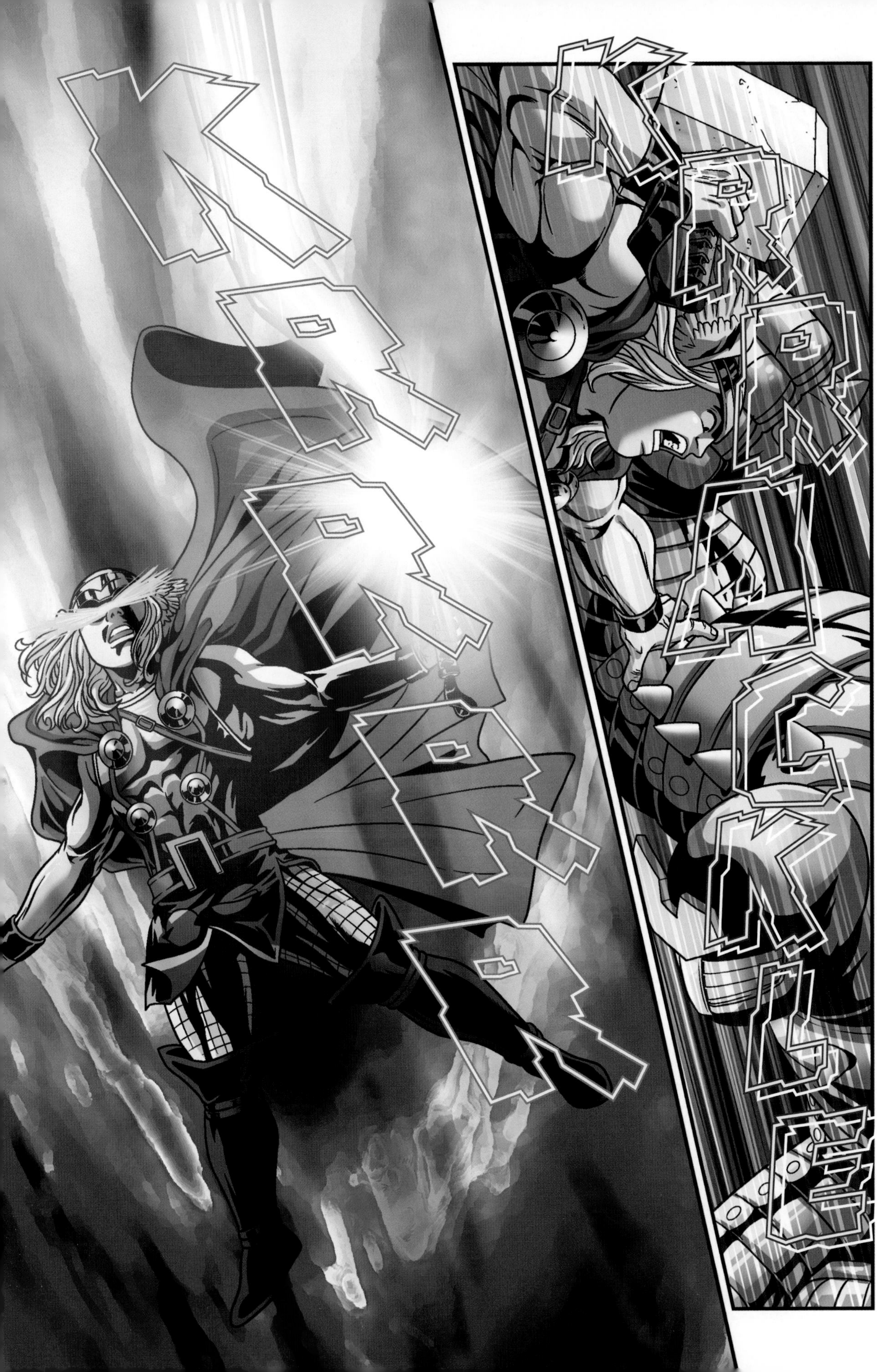
KRRRRR
KRRACKLE

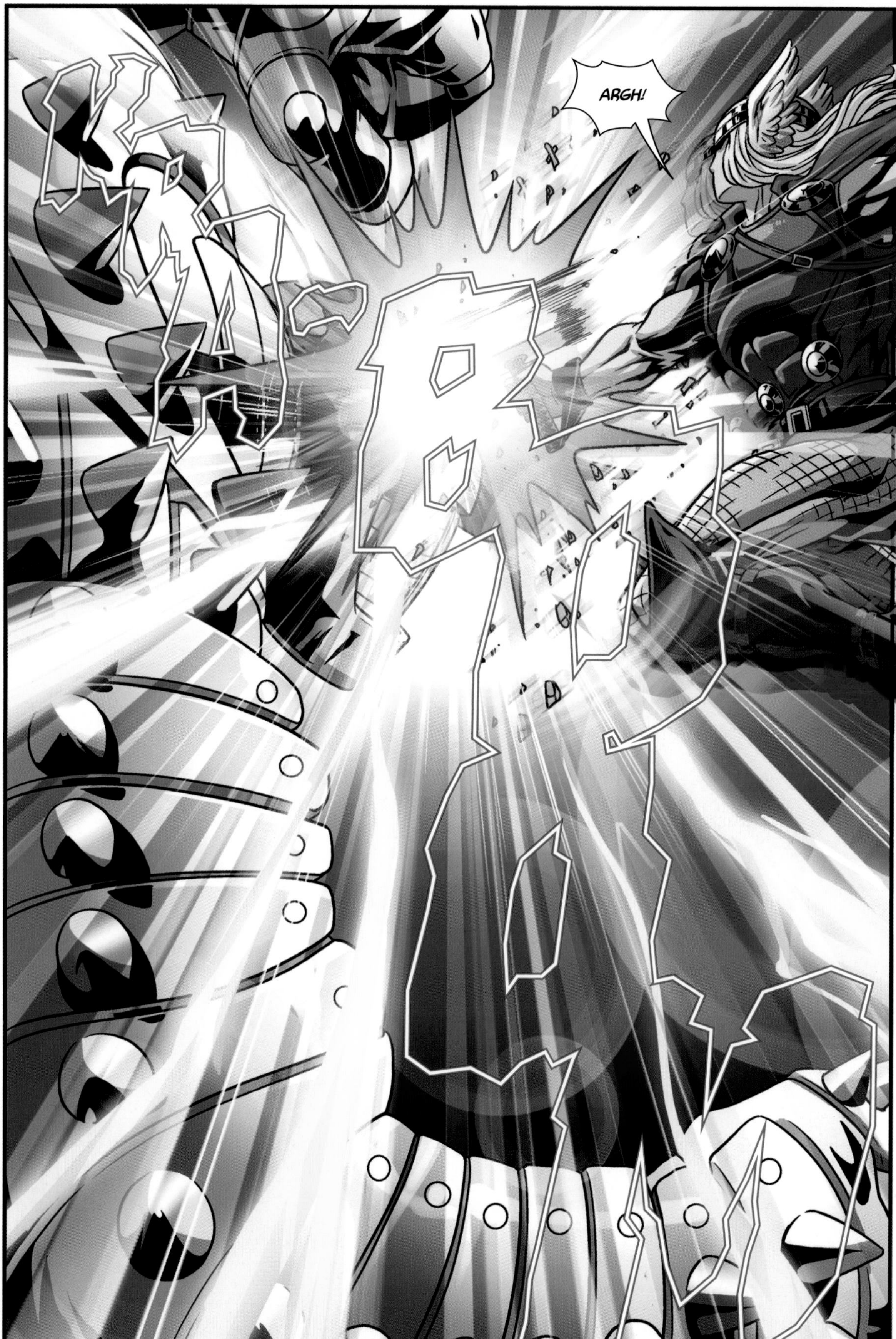
KA-BOOM
ARGH!

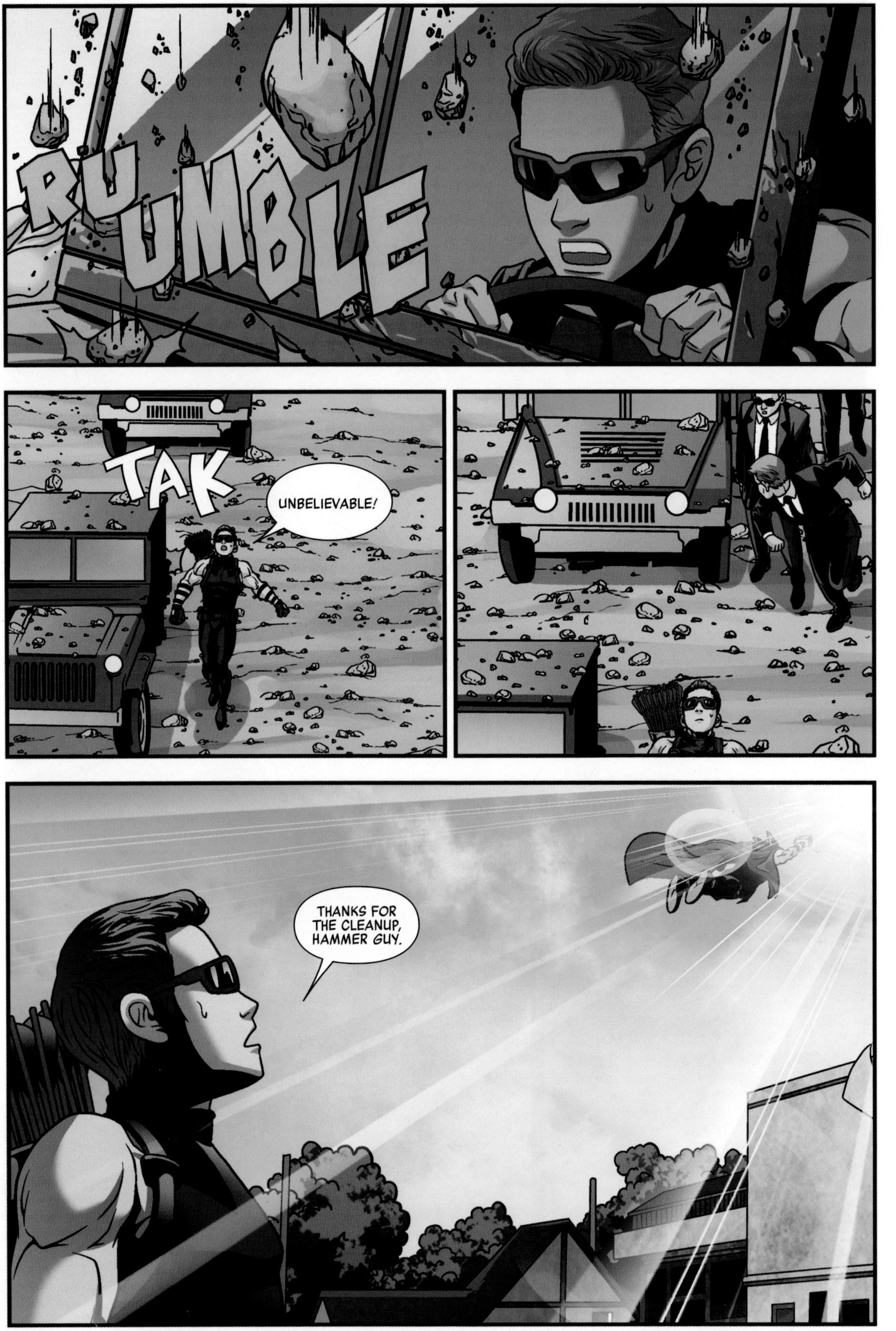
RUUMBLE
TAK
UNBELIEVABLE!
THANKS FOR THE CLEANUP, HAMMER GUY.

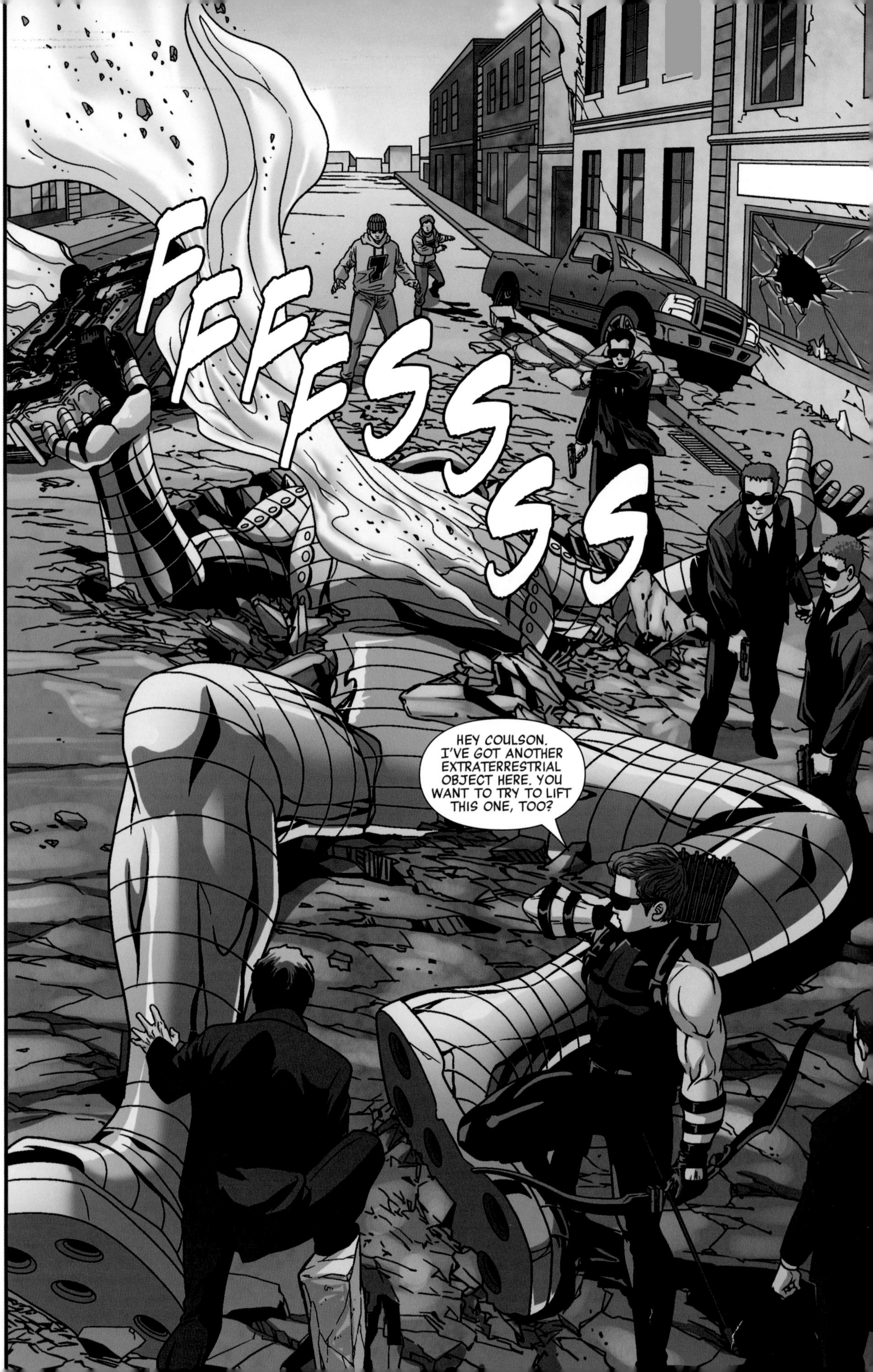
FFFFSSSSS
HEY COULSON. I'VE GOT ANOTHER EXTRATERRESTRIAL OBJECT HERE. YOU WANT TO TRY TO LIFT THIS ONE, TOO?

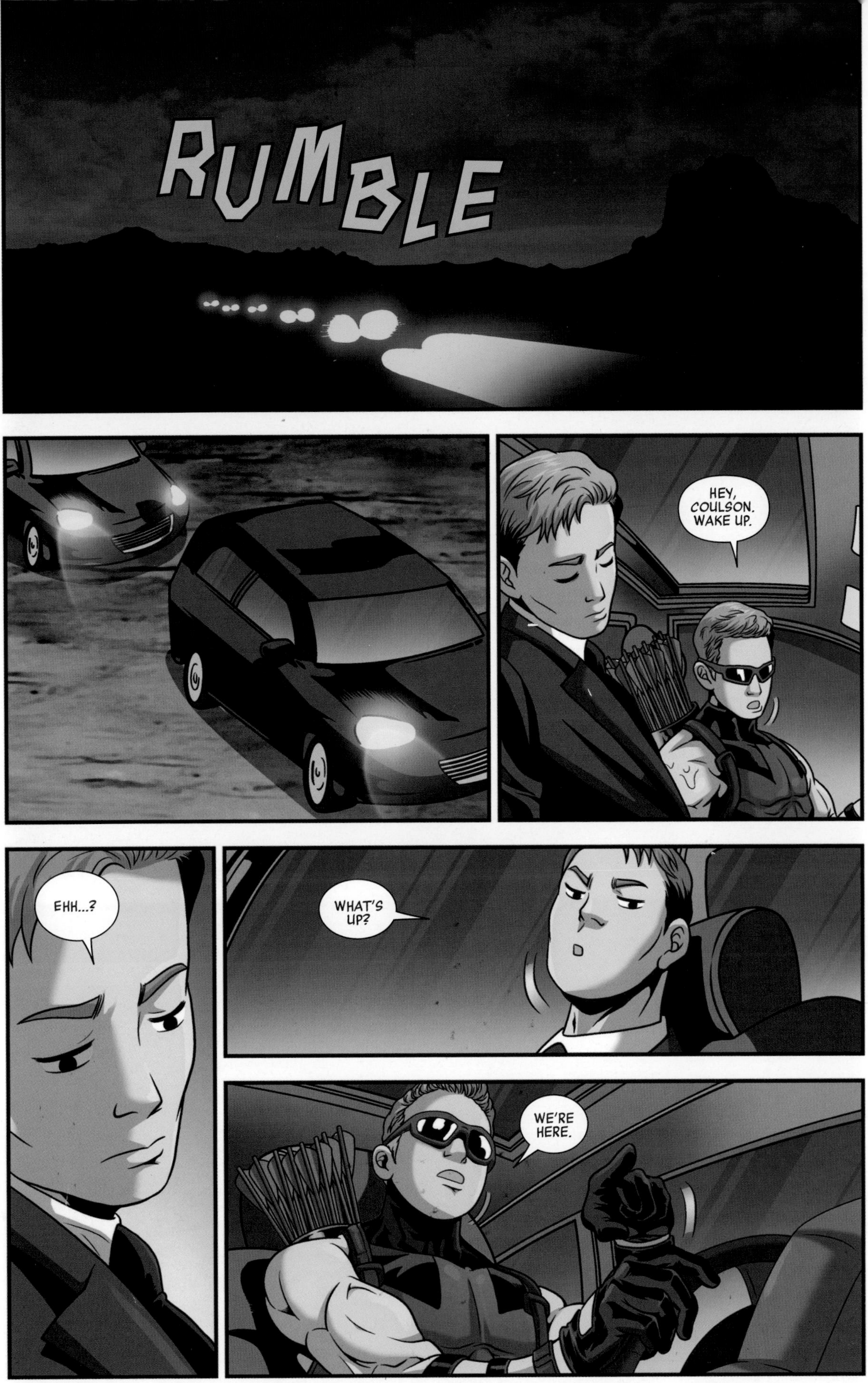
RUMBLE
HEY, COULSON. WAKE UP.
EHH...?
WHAT'S UP?
WE'RE HERE.

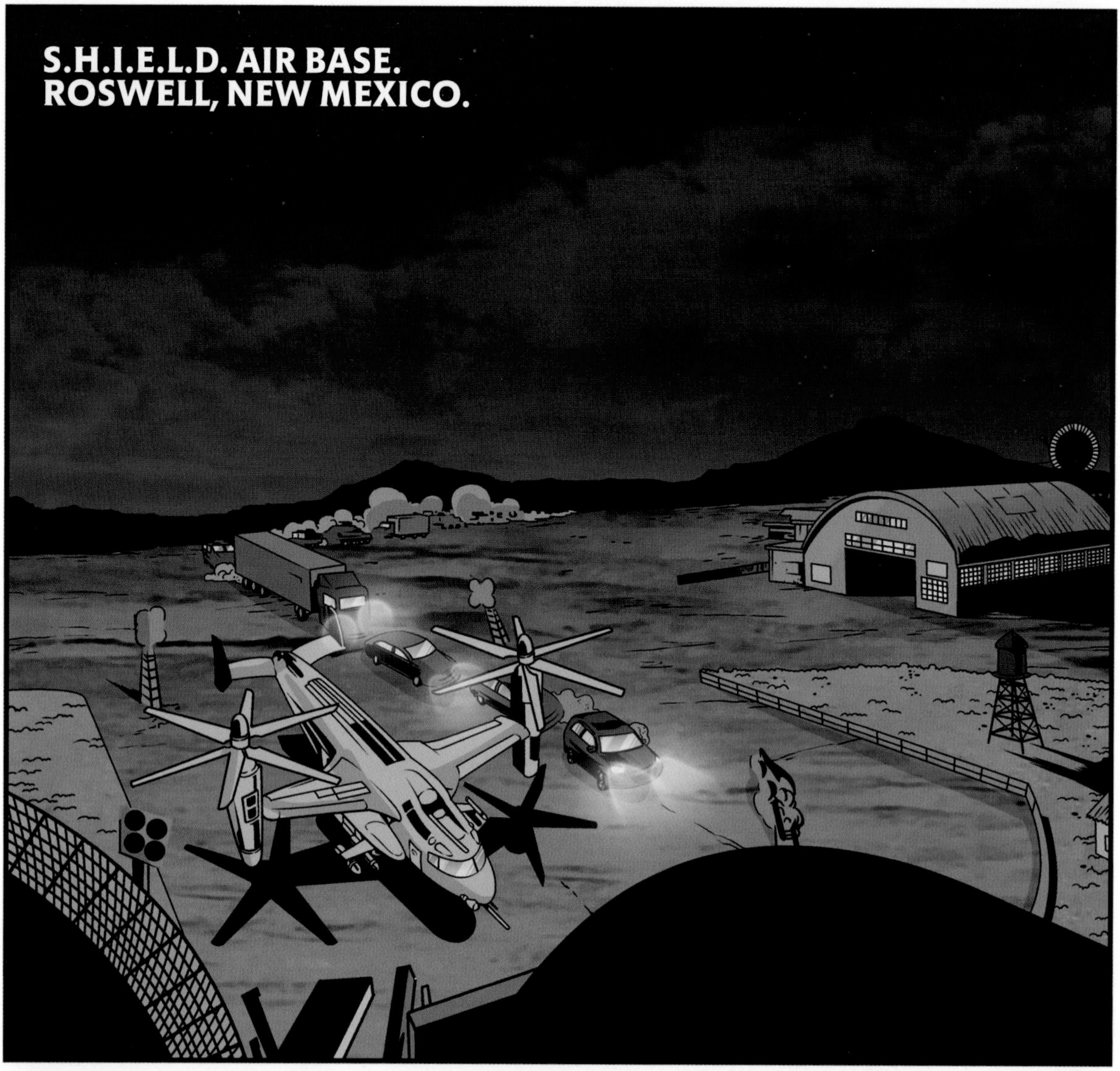
S.H.I.E.L.D. AIR BASE.
ROSWELL, NEW MEXICO.

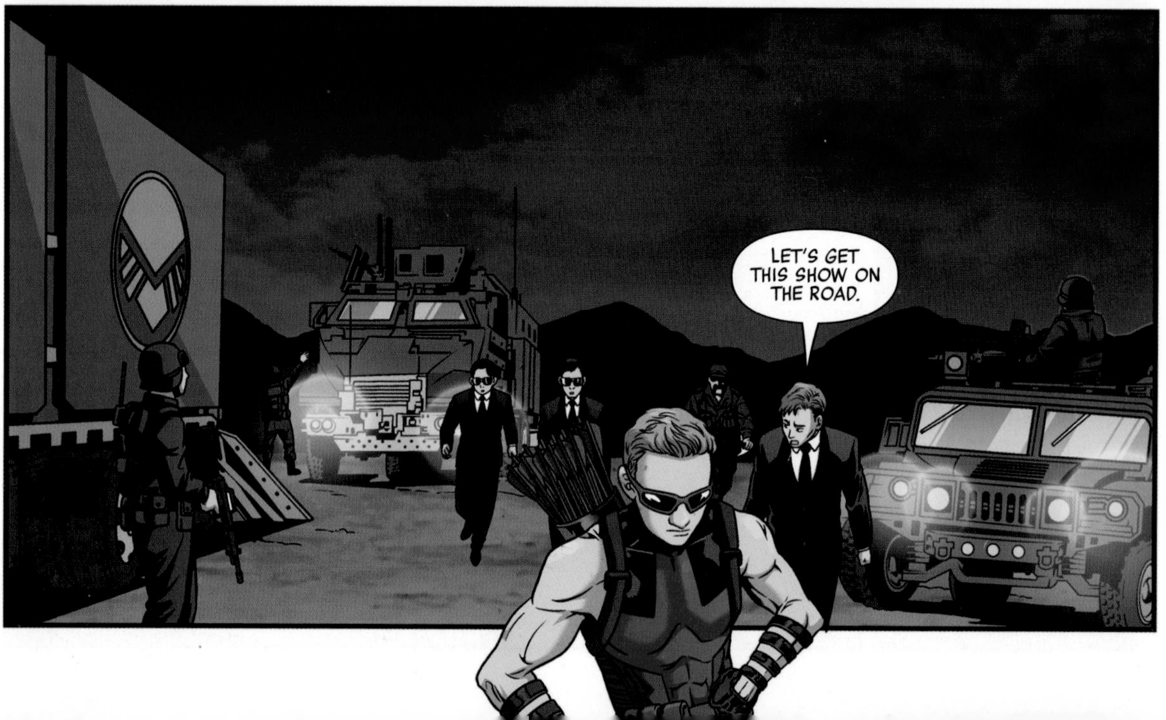
LET'S GET THIS SHOW ON THE ROAD.

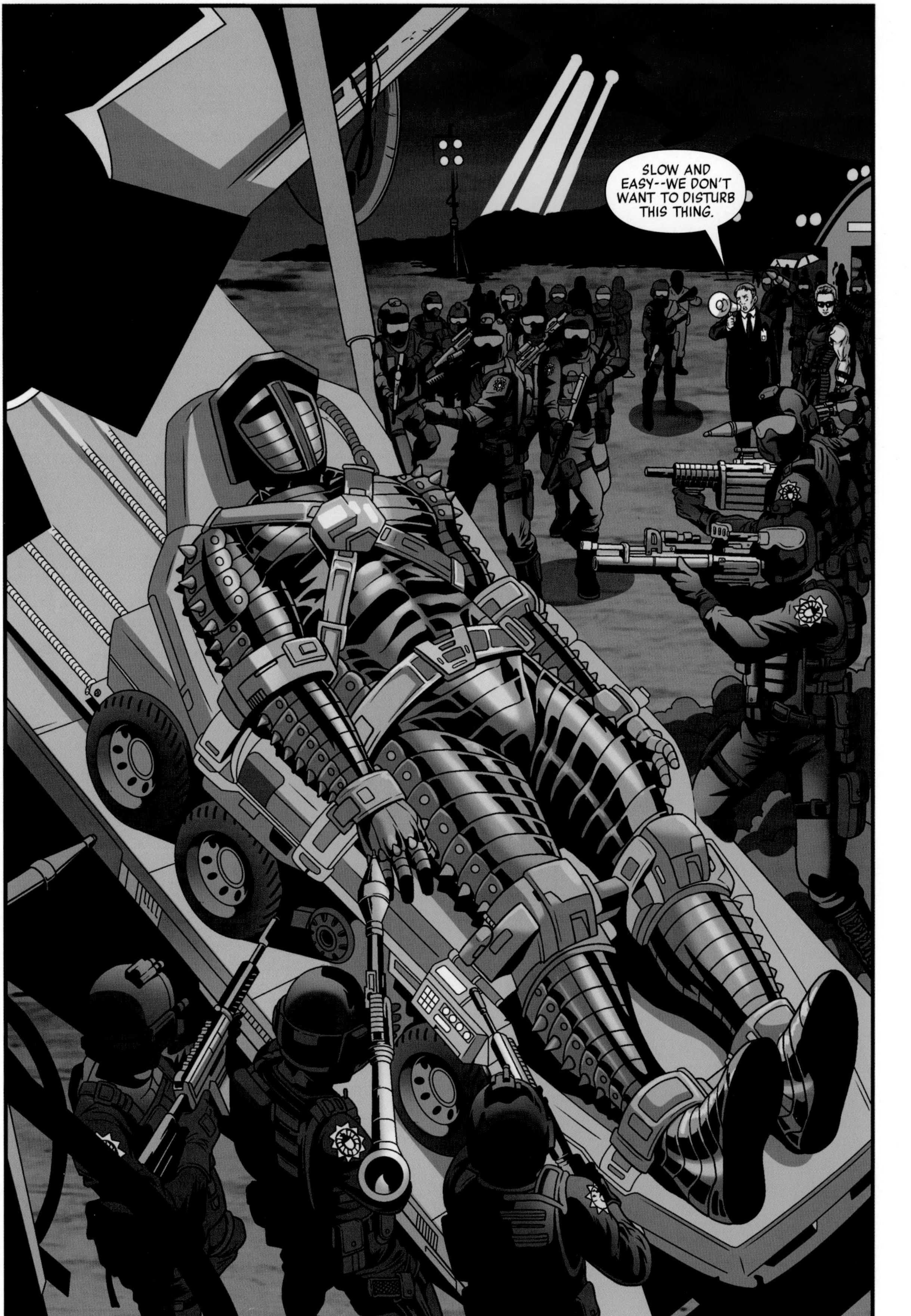
SLOW AND EASY--WE DON'T WANT TO DISTURB THIS THING.

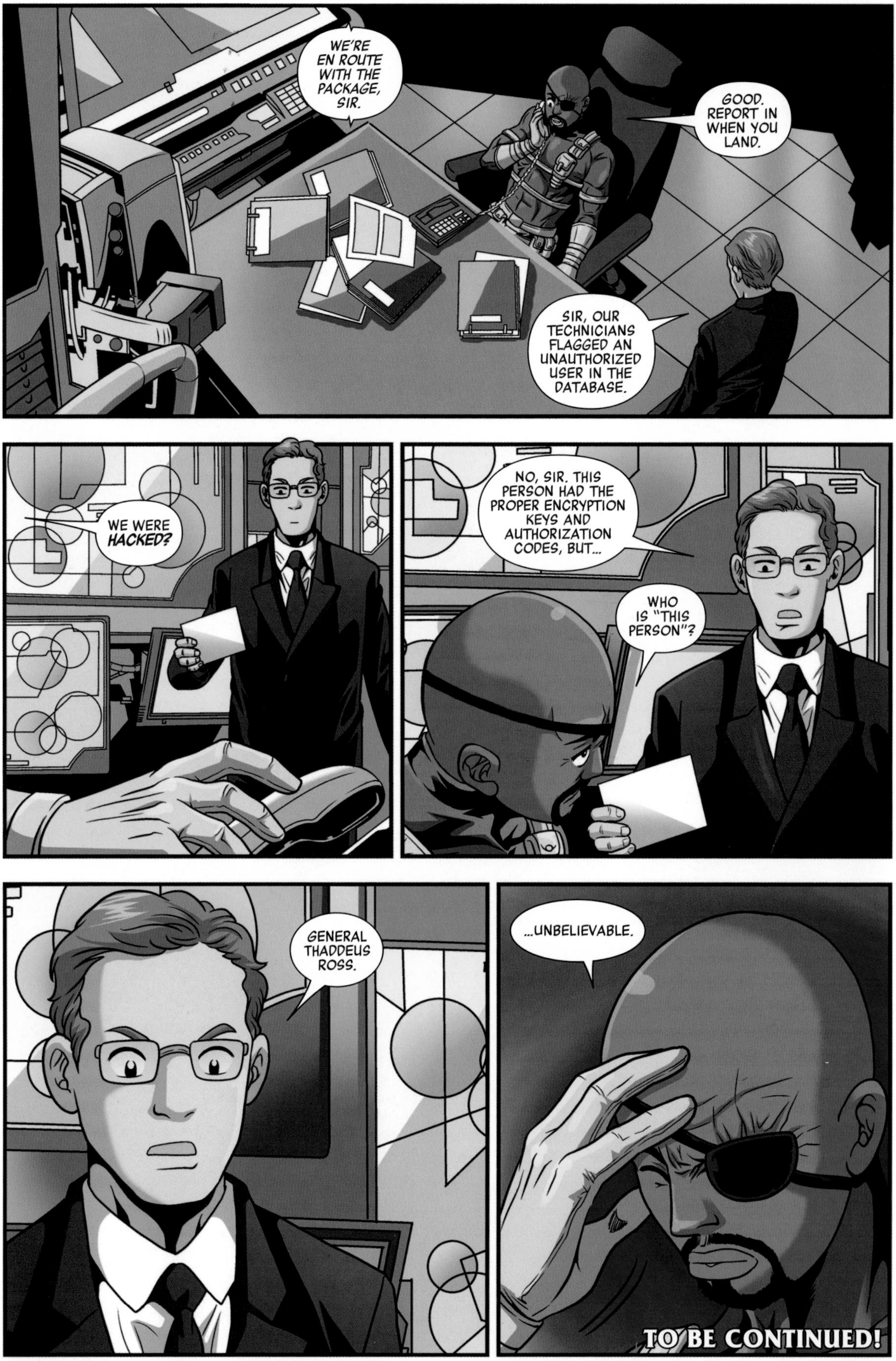
WE'RE EN ROUTE WITH THE PACKAGE, SIR.
GOOD. REPORT IN WHEN YOU LAND.
SIR, OUR TECHNICIANS FLAGGED AN UNAUTHORIZED USER IN THE DATABASE.
WE WERE *HACKED?*
NO, SIR. THIS PERSON HAD THE PROPER ENCRYPTION KEYS AND AUTHORIZATION CODES, BUT...
WHO IS "THIS PERSON"?
GENERAL THADDEUS ROSS.
...UNBELIEVABLE.
TO BE CONTINUED!

AVENGERS K
ASSEMBLING THE AVENGERS

COLLECT THEM ALL!

Set of 7 Hardcover Books ISBN: 978-1-5321-4146-1

AVENGERS K #1
ASSEMBLING THE AVENGERS
MARVEL

Hardcover Book ISBN
978-1-5321-4147-8

AVENGERS K #2
ASSEMBLING THE AVENGERS
MARVEL

Hardcover Book ISBN
978-1-5321-4148-5

AVENGERS K #3
ASSEMBLING THE AVENGERS
MARVEL

Hardcover Book ISBN
978-1-5321-4149-2

AVENGERS K #4
ASSEMBLING THE AVENGERS
MARVEL

Hardcover Book ISBN
978-1-5321-4150-8

AVENGERS K #5
ASSEMBLING THE AVENGERS
MARVEL

Hardcover Book ISBN
978-1-5321-4151-5

AVENGERS K #6
ASSEMBLING THE AVENGERS
MARVEL

Hardcover Book ISBN
978-1-5321-4152-2

AVENGERS K #7
ASSEMBLING THE AVENGERS
MARVEL

Hardcover Book ISBN
978-1-5321-4153-9

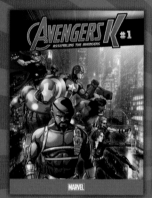